Dear Parents:

Congratulations! Your child is taking the first steps on an exciting journey. The destination? Independent reading!

STEP INTO READING® will help your child get there. The program offers five steps to reading success. Each step includes fun stories and colorful art or photographs. In addition to original fiction and books with favorite characters, there are Step into Reading Non-Fiction Readers, Phonics Readers and Boxed Sets, Sticker Readers, and Comic Readers—a complete literacy program with something to interest every child.

Learning to Read, Step by Step!

Ready to Read   Preschool–Kindergarten
• big type and easy words • rhyme and rhythm • picture clues
For children who know the alphabet and are eager to begin reading.

Reading with Help   Preschool–Grade 1
• basic vocabulary • short sentences • simple stories
For children who recognize familiar words and sound out new words with help.

Reading on Your Own   Grades 1–3
• engaging characters • easy-to-follow plots • popular topics
For children who are ready to read on their own.

Reading Paragraphs   Grades 2–3
• challenging vocabulary • short paragraphs • exciting stories
For newly independent readers who read simple sentences with confidence.

Ready for Chapters   Grades 2–4
• chapters • longer paragraphs • full-color art
For children who want to take the plunge into chapter books but still like colorful pictures.

STEP INTO READING® is designed to give every child a successful reading experience. The grade levels are only guides; children will progress through the steps at their own speed, developing confidence in their reading.

Remember, a lifetime love of reading starts with a single step!

DreamWorks Trolls © 2017 DreamWorks Animation LLC. All Rights Reserved. Published in the United States by Random House Children's Books, a division of Penguin Random House LLC, 1745 Broadway, New York, NY 10019, and in Canada by Penguin Random House Canada Limited, Toronto, in conjunction with DreamWorks Animation LLC.

Visit us on the Web!
StepIntoReading.com
randomhousekids.com

Educators and librarians, for a variety of teaching tools, visit us at RHTeachersLibrarians.com

ISBN 978-0-399-55870-2 (trade) — ISBN 978-0-399-55871-9 (lib. bdg.)
ISBN 978-0-399-55872-6 (ebook)

Printed in the United States of America
10 9 8 7 6 5 4 3 2 1

DREAMWORKS

TROLLS

POPPY and BRANCH'S
BIG ADVENTURE

by Mona Miller

Random House 🏠 New York

I'm King Peppy.
This is the story
of how my daughter
became queen.

Her name is Poppy,

and she is the

happiest, singing-est Troll

in Troll Village.

Her friend Branch
was a gray Troll.
He did not like
to dance, sing,
or even hug!

He warned Poppy

to be quiet,

or our enemies,

the Bergens,

might hear.

Who are the Bergens?
The Bergens were once
unhappy giants
who lived in
Bergen Town.
They liked to groan
and complain.

Worst of all, they thought
that eating Trolls
was the only thing
that would ever
make them happy.

When a Bergen named Chef
found Troll Village,
she took many
of Poppy's friends.

Poppy bravely set off
into the big, wide world
to find and save them!

Her journey was not easy.

There was beauty.

And there was also danger.

But Poppy never
gave up hope!

On the way, she was attacked
by big, fuzzy spiders!
Why does everyone
want to eat Trolls?

Poppy was wrapped
in a ball of spiderweb.
She seemed like a goner
for sure!

That was when Branch
finally showed up.
He rescued her
from the spiders!

Poppy always knew
Branch would come.
She thought they
made a great team.

17

Together they continued
through the forest.
It was a long trip.
Poppy talked about
her rescue plan.

Branch was willing

to help Poppy

save their friends . . .

. . . but he was not so sure
her plan would work.

Poppy had a way

of looking at things

on the bright side.

Branch only saw danger.

Poppy and Branch
eventually found
some tunnels that led
to Bergen Town.

But they did not know
which one to take.

They met a new friend
named Cloud Guy,
who offered to show them
the correct path.

He helped, but first
he teased Branch
by making him give
hugs and fist bumps.

Poppy and Branch
finally made it into
the Bergen castle—
only to be caught
by Chef!

Chef was going to cook

all the Trolls

for King Gristle!

For the first time ever,
Poppy lost all hope—
and all her color.
The other Trolls did, too.

They became gray, like Branch.

But then something

amazing happened.

Branch started to sing!

Poppy got her colors back,

and Branch wasn't gray anymore!

Then all the Trolls

became colorful again.

Singing had made

their true colors appear!

After that, Poppy and Branch
showed the Bergens
that there were better ways
to be happy than by
eating Trolls.

So we danced and sang
and made Poppy our queen!
But I bet our adventures
are just beginning!